Nicole's Journey

ARNITA INGRAM

PAGE PUBLISHING, INC.
Conneaut Lake, PA

First originally published by Page Publishing 2021

ISBN 978-1-6624-1309-4 (pbk)
ISBN 978-1-6624-1310-0 (digital)

Printed in the United States of America

Introduction

BEEP... BEEP... BEEP... beep... The sound of a discharged fire alarm followed by the sound of coughing filled the air in the one-bedroom apartment building. The beeping subsided then followed by the sound of a smoke-filled lung coughing heavily. "What the..." Cough, cough, cough, "what the fuck are you in there doing!" Isaiah yelled repeatedly while rushing out of bed to open all the windows in the bedroom. He then proceeded to grab one of the chairs tucked into the desk by the wall and climbed up to reset the fire alarm. "I swear you can't even do simple shit! Why do I have to wake up to you burning food again?"

Another person was heard coughing then answered in reply to his statement, a feminine cough. "I swear, I don't know why I even bother. You don't appreciate shit I do for your ass!" A woman's voice yelled from what appeared to be the kitchen. Nicole was not what you would call gifted culinary-wise. She stood in front of the sink, running the faucet into a smoking skillet while trying to salvage what little food remained unburnt. At first glance, you wouldn't be surprised by that either. She was light-skinned, and her left arm was covered with a sleeve of various roses and other tattoos. She had hazel eyes and full lips, which she constantly licked when frustrated or upset. She looked like one of those women who had everything handed to them all their lives, so cooking was the last thing you would think she knew how to do. And you would be right!

Isaiah walked into the kitchen rubbing his left eye and looking around the confined kitchen/living room space. "Now the whole house smells like smoke. Why are you messing around in here when you know damn well you can't cook?" He walked over to Nicole and asked again, "Nikki, I know damn well you hear me talking to you." Nicole, still facing the sink, stood quietly, gritting her teeth then licking her bottom lip. She gripped the now-cooled skillet sitting in the sink and started fantasizing about using all the force in her left arm and throwing it at his head. She couldn't stand Isaiah some days; he was the type of guy that each of your friends tell you to stop messing with because you deserve better. But for the life of you, it was always something about him that keeps you there. He was an asshole most of the time—always criticizing something she said or did, asking two thousand questions about where she was and who she was with when she wasn't right under his nose. He was jealous, immature, ungrateful, and unambitious, but there was something that wouldn't allow her to walk out of that door and on to better. She knew exactly what it was too—the sex.

Chapter 1

THE RELATIONSHIP STARTED off as any normal one would. Nicole and Isaiah happened to be at one of the biggest birthday bashes Chicago has ever seen. One of Chicago greatest rappers, Kanye West, celebrated his birthday at a well-known club in the downtown area. Isaiah saw Nicole from across the room sitting with a couple of her friends, and with a little liquid courage, he decided to approach her. She had her hair in long curls, and she wore a sleeveless shirt that was just long enough to cover her butt in her black leggings. Now Isaiah was a smooth-type dude starting out. He had long braids, dimples, was very chiseled, and had a way of talking any women into wanting him bad. As he approached Nicole, he started to get nervous and wondering if he was making the right move. At first glanced, he saw her as the type who really didn't take a lot of shit but, at the same time, a good girl trying to be bad. He got to the middle of the room, and they made eye contact. As Kanye West performed his "Can't Tell Me Nothing" smash, he spoke to her for the first time, with a pretty boy smirk, "Hey, miss lady," his deep voice sounding like a heavy bass. She replied with a simple hi as she turned back to the stage. "If you give me the time to get to know you, I'm sure it will be worth your time." "Ha! Don't come and use the same line on me as you've used on every girl in this room," Nicole eyerolled. Isaiah knew he would have to work just a little harder to get what he wanted. He went for a second try saying, "If—" She cut him off. "If, if, if… Don't sound too sure about yourself, huh? If *if* was a fifth, we will all be drunk by now." he laughed and came with an even better line. "I'm going to be the one you leave the club with and spend the rest of your life with." "Confident, I see. So much better than before," Nicole replied.

As the bartender came around, Isaiah picked up two shots of patron and tipped the waiter. Isaiah handed her one and told her, "Let's toast to the night you won't forget, or is it the ones you can't remember?" as he chuckled. After a couple shots of alcohol and an amazing concert, before you knew it, they were pulling up to his condo. As they entered the elevator up to the twentieth floor, he kissed her neck gently over and over again.

She glazed into his eyes, trying to hold out but knowing she wanted it just as bad as he did. *Ding*, the door opens. They walked two doors down and entered his apartment. The view from his balcony has a great look over the Chicago skyline. As the warm summer breeze hit her skin, she took a deep breath then exhaled.

As she stood out on the balcony with her eyes closed, hand gripping the guard rail, she began contemplating the decision of sleeping with this man or not. "You just meet this man. You don't know anything about him nor what he does nor what he's about. Fucking him is out of the question." Nicole repeated this statement in her mind over and over, but her body was not listening in any type of way. It had been months since the last time she has some dick, and passing up this opportunity seemed out of the question. The level of frustration she was feeling was on an entire new level, higher than anything she had felt before. She felt a sharp pain in her lip as she realized she had been digging her teeth into it for an unknown amount of time.

She heard Isaiah moving around inside of the house. "What do you have a taste for?" he asked from the kitchen. *Shit, some dick*, she thought to herself. She smirked, her back still turned away from the house, without realizing she hadn't answered. "Umm, I'll take whatever you have," she smirked again. Isaiah walked onto the balcony with a bottle and two glasses filled with ice. Nicole's eyes focused on the glasses in his hands then slowly edged to his chest. Trying her hardest to keep her vision from dropping any lower but as if her body fell from her control, she blinked and realized she was staring directly at his dick. "Thirsty?" "Huh," she blurted out. "I said, are you thirsty?" "Oh, yeah, I'll take a drink." *Okay, you need to calm yourself down,* she thought to herself. But shit, this opportunity was looking too damn good to pass up. Okay, fuck it. If he has the balls to make a move, you fuck him. If he just sits there talking that good shit, then you get his number and talk to him in a few days.

Nicole went inside and took a seat on the couch as he followed behind her. She looked up at him. "So what made you finally say something to me? I peeped you staring at me for a minute." She uncrossed her legs, showing off the outlining of the red lace thong, smirked, then looked up at him awaiting his answer. Isaiah looked down then sat in a chair across the table from her. *Okay, you got her back to the house, now how are you going to fuck?* Isaiah thought to himself while taking another sip. *Damn, she looks good as fuck, and she's showing off that thong on some low-key shit. I know she wants this dick, but how do I play this?* Snapping himself out of his thoughts, he took a sip of the patron in his glass and proceeded to answer. "Well, as soon as I got there, I looked in your direction, and from that moment on, I had it set in my mind we would leave together." He looked at her and smiled. "Oh, so you just knew you had me in the bag, huh?" "Well, nothing is a sure thing, but I figured, if you gave me the chance to shoot my shot, I could make it happen." Isaiah got up from his seat, walked around the table, then sat next to Nicole. *Hmm, okay, let's see what you're about,* Nicole thought to herself. He sat his glass on the table then took hers out of her hand and placed it next to his. Edging himself closer, he leaned in and ran his tongue across her earlobe then slid down to her neck. He pressed his lips against her skin then opened his mouth and started biting on her neck. *Fuck! How does he know my spot? This Man just met me tonight.* Nicole's bottom lip faded from a pink tint to light purple from the pressure her teeth were applying to it. She forced herself to let go but then accidently let a moan slip from her mouth. His hands lifted her shirt up, just enough to get his hands under it. Before another moan could escape, he had already slipped her red laced bra off and thrown it on the floor. *Damn, he works quick. This might be a bad idea. Okay, if I'm going to get the fuck out of here. It's got to be now or never.* He felt her hips raising like she was about to stand up. *Okay, now or never,* she thought to herself. His hands left her tit in seconds and ran straight between her legs, massaging her pussy lips from the outside of her leggings. *Fuck. Game over.*

Nicole immediately fell back into her seat and opened her legs as wide as they could spread. *I'm not about to let this man show me up.* She looked down at his lap and unbuckled his belt then ripped the zipper down and watched it hanging half off. Going right through his boxer, her hand ran down and gripped his already-hard dick. *Shit, this man has to be ten inches easy.* She stroked it slowly while moving her neck out of his mouth then shoving her tongue down his throat. Nicole grabbed the back of his head and guided it down to her chest, watching as Isaiah rolled his tongue over each of her nipples then licked down her stomach. Isaiah lifted her legs up and took her leggings off then

11

sucked on each of her inner thighs. She looked down at him. "Show me you know how to use that tongue on this pussy," Nicole said while letting out another soft moan. He gave her a look of confidence then slid his tongue inside of her pussy lips. "Oh fuck!" she let it out as her eyes rolled to the back of her head and her hand pushed his head deeper between her legs. *His fucking tongue has me melting in his mouth*, she thought to herself while trying to hold on as the feeling was taking over her. He gripped both of her legs and pinned them down so she couldn't move. Spinning his tongue inside of her as she squirmed trying to get away and regain some control, her back started to arch as she felt herself about to cum. She dug her nails in his back then let out a loud scream and lost it as his tongue wrapped around her clit. With all the strength she had left, she pushed him onto the table in front of them then pulled off his pants and threw them to the other side of the room. She then reached out and grabbed his dick still on hard and started stroking it again while licking the shaft up and down and sucking just the tip. Rolling her tongue across the head, she looked up and watched Isaiah's head fall back and his arm slowly raise then rest on the back of her neck. He began guiding her head up and down his dick. Nicole looked up again then slapped his hands away and, in the blink of an eye, started to deep throat every inch of his dick. *Fuck, she knows what she's doing*, he thought. She tightened her grip and proceeded to suck up and down, speeding up the pace and making sure every part of his dick was soaking wet. She felt him cringe up and knew it was time for the main event.

Before Isaiah could even look up and see why she had stopped giving some of the best head he ever gotten, she was already lowering her hips down on to his dick. He watched as his entire dick disappeared inside her then used all the force in his right hand to grip the back of her ass. Nicole was an expert at riding. She knew how to work the dick from the inside out. She bounced her hips on his waist, going straight up in the air and all the way back down. Her back perfectly arched, ass sitting up as his dick went in and out, but Isaiah was not going for being the submissive one any longer. Nicole closed her eyes and, in that instant, felt herself being lifted up. He picked her up then walked over to the nearest wall and pinned her to it. Raising her legs up until they were rested on his arms, he shoved himself back in her already-soaked wet pussy lips and pushing as deep inside of her as he could fit. Fighting past any resistance he was getting inside of her, he wanted to make sure she could feel him in her stomach. Breathing heavily, he dug his teeth back into her neck, and immediately Nicole let out an even louder scream with no hope of containing any more. At this point, she gave in as she took over.

His strokes almost seemed like he had prior knowledge about her; every direction he thrusted in was almost the perfect spot to be hit at that moment. *Fuck! Fuck! Fuck! How much deeper can his ass get inside of me?* Nicole tried her best to hold her composure, but with no success, he was fucking her like he owned her body. She felt herself getting lightheaded then being lifted once again, but now she was being bent over the couch.

Isaiah lifted her legs up then spread them open and shoved his dick back inside of her. He grabbed her waist then wrapped his hand around her neck and pulled her back, sticking it inside of her completely. Nicole snapped herself out of her sex high and started throwing her ass back on his dick while gripping the couch. She clenched and forced her pussy lips to grip his dick from the inside. His strokes started to speed up as his breathing got heavier and harder. *I know he's close*, Nicole thought to herself. Isaiah gripped Nicole's ass and dug in as deep as possible, going faster with every passing second he felt himself about to cum. "Fuck, I'm about to nut," he said, and Nicole responded with "Give it to me then!" He grabbed the back of her hair and pulled it hard then smacked her ass and shot his load inside of her. *Shit, damn girl!* Nicole collapsed then looked back at Isaiah standing there sweating, and all she could do was ask herself, *Why did you just fuck this man who you've known for all of six hours. The fuck were you thinking?* All guilty pleasure aside, she couldn't ignore one thing: that was some of the best sex she had experience, and she was hooked. She may not have known him for long, but damn, she was going to now.

Chapter 2

In life, there will be occasions where we encounter people that feel as if they are crafted especially for us, with the indescribable ways they make us feel or crazy things they have the power to make us do. The problem is, sometimes, we can be blinded by these intense emotions, and that is when we are at our most vulnerable. Nicole was in love head over heels with no doubt in her mind, and there was nothing on this earth she wouldn't do for this man. Unfortunately, Isaiah was fully aware of this and had no problem exploiting it. Whether it be buying him something extravagant, taking him somewhere, or ignoring some of his newly unattractive behavior, Nicole would do it at the lift of a finger. It was about a year into the relationship before things began to get a little rocky between the two. Isaiah had a real possessive streak in him that he made it his business to know Nicole's whereabouts at all times. If she took too long to reply to a text message, she would immediately receive a call interrogating her about where she was or who she was with. She would get a full third degree when going out with a few friends or even out having lunch with someone. There was one friend in particular whom Isaiah absolutely could not stand, and he had no problem making it known to Nicole and to her. Isaiah hated Nicole's best friend Kiesha because she's that one single friend that Nicole had who essentially lived a promiscuous life-style and forever tried to get Nicole to do the same. She was the one who loved to go out and have a good time, lived by the "go with the flow" attitude, and wanted someone there to do the same. The first time she was unofficially introduced, she left a poor first impression on Isaiah, which was due to the fact that she was unaware she would be meeting him and let her mouth run off without thinking, like she usually does.

It was a Friday, and Nicole was standing in front of the bathroom mirror applying makeup to her eyes when her phone, which was sitting on the left side of the sink, began to ring. Nicole picked it up, and another person's voice was heard on the other end of the phone asking was she ready yet. "I'm almost done, relax," she replied. "You said that over an hour ago," Kiesha said. "Something came up, and it set me back a little. Just come upstairs." "Ugh. If we are late to this party, I'm beating your ass." Nicole hung up the phone then continued to apply the makeup. A minute or so passed, and then a knock was heard at the door. "Just a minute!" Nicole yelled as she rushed to the door to let Kiesha in. "Bitch, come on! I swear you always take forever!" Kiesha yelled. "I'm coming, just got to put on my pumps." When Isaiah heard Kiesha's voice, he immediately walked out the room to see what was going on. "So you just gon' leave without saying bye and with Kiesha of all people?" "It is not like that. I just put on my shoes. I was coming in there anyway to put on some perfume. We're going down to SawTooth for a little bit. I'll call you when I get there and when I leave," Nicole said as if she was tired of explaining her every move. Isaiah walked into the room and closed the door without responding, knowing she would follow. Nicole walked in and asked him what his problem. "Nothing. Just go out, have a good time, and come back to me just as faithful as you left," he said. She yelled bye, then kissed him on his lips, grabbed her perfume and lipstick, and rushed out the house with Kiesha.

As they walked out the door, Nicole looked at Kiesha and asked her to not start with her and "Let's just have a good time." "Good time is all I needed to hear. Imma get you so fucked up you're going to forget about the fight you just had." They both started laughing as the cab driver pulled off around the corner. As they entered the club, they made their way to VIP, where the birthday girl, Crystal, and a couple others were already turning up. After about thirty minutes into the club, Nicole bumped into and old Jovan, who has been crushing on her since grammar school. Whenever Jovan saw her, he had to go and shoot his shot with the hope that one day, his wish will come true. "Hey, Nikki. I see your man let you off the leash," Jovan said while giggling. Nicole smiled as she told him to get her a drink. "No problem. I'll be right back," he said. Even through Nicole was madly in love with Isaiah, it was a good feeling knowing someone still wanted her for her and was not trying to control her. "I see Jovan is back to his old ways, and you should let him show you that he's not all talk and really worth it in the bedroom," Kiesha said as she sipped her drink. "Here you go, always looking for a new man for me. Jovan knows where he stands and will not cross that line." Not saying that Nicole hasn't thought about it, but she was just not ready to risk what her and Isaiah had. A few drinks and one hell of a party later, Isaiah began to blow up her phone. She walked to the bathroom to call him back after realizing she missed three calls already. "Hey, baby, what's up!" "I thought you was supposed to call me when you got there! It's been two hours, ain't got a call yet!' Isaiah said, shouting on the other end of the phone. "Sorry. I'll make it up to you when I get home. We are finishing up here. Will be home in about another hour or so." "All right, I'll be here," he said then hung up the phone. "Nikki, I thought I lost you in the crowd. Been looking all over for my dance." Nicole smirked as she grabbed Jovan by the collar and led him to the dance floor. As Nicole grind on Jovan, he grabbed her waist and softly kissed her neck as if that one night she belonged to him. Nicole let the music take her mind into another zone, and she danced liked there was no tomorrow. As Jovan got his usual feels, she imagined what her life could be with him—marriage, luxury, maybe even a kid. "Nikki, Nikki, you don't hear me talking to you!" Kiesha tried to yell over the music. Jovan gave Nicole a shake, to wake her out of her fairytale daydream. "Girl, come on, it's like four in the morning! I'm drunk, and if we don't leave now, I might punch a bitch!" Kiesha yelled while grabbing Nicole's arm. "All right, I'll meet you outside. Let me say bye to Crystal and shit." "Make it quick. I'm waiting," she said while walking away. Nicole and Jovan walked over to the VIP section, and she gave Crystal a hug and mingled for a quick second with everyone else. As she processed downstairs, Jovan called her name. "Wait a minute, I got something for you." She stopped and turned around as he scurried to her side. "Hold your arm out," he told her. As she held her arm out, he reached in his pocket and pulled out a diamond bracelet and placed it around her wrist. "Just a little something you can remember me by until we bump into each other again," he said. "Now you know that you don't have to give me anything, and what am I supposed to tell Isaiah?" "If he asks, tell him it's from an old friend, nothing more nothing less," he said right before he kissed her. Nicole felt a spark, one that has been missing for months now. "I got to go. Kiesha is waiting. I'll text you," she said as she rushed out the club in somewhat embarrassment.

"Girl, what took you so long? You damn near got left" Kiesha slurred as she tried to get her words out. "Jovan kissed me and gave me a diamond bracelet. I don't know how I feel about that." "Well, did you get butterflies in your stomach?" "Yeah, and they're still here." "Well, you know exactly how to feel about that," Kiesha added. As the cab driver pulled up to Nicole's house, she gave Kiesha a hug and made sure to put the bracelet into her purse before walking in the house. As the door opened, Isaiah was sitting on the couch with a drink in his cup and watching ESPN. "Hey, baby, how was your night?" he asked. "Fine, I had a good time. Crystal enjoyed herself." "That's good, but your ass was still hanging out with that groupie Kiesha, so I know all was around a bunch of dudes!" he shouted. "It was a club—dudes, bitches, etc. You have to know, I will never cheat on you, so relax," Nicole said while undressing. "How about you help me relax?" Nicole walked over to the couch and threw her shirt across the room. She slung one leg across Isaiah's lap and unbuckled his belt then pulled down his pants just enough to get his dick out. He went to grab for her breast, but she quickly pushed his hands down. "No touching. You're supposed to be relaxing, so just sit back, keep your hands to yourself, and enjoy." She slowly eased onto his dick and softly moaned. As she started to ride his dick faster and faster, she closed her eyes and began to grab her breasts and imagined that she was riding Jovan's dick. Isaiah couldn't resist, so he grabbed her ass and guided her up and down, trying to control her speed. Nicole didn't let him take over. She kept going at her own pace while biting her bottom lip. Isaiah gave in and leaned back on the couch and put his hands over his head. She began to shake as she can feel her body ready to explode. She put one hand on the couch and licked his neck. Isaiah moved his head and stuck his tongue down her throat and slapped her ass. She could no longer control it, and her juices exploded all over his lap and the couch, then she let out a sigh of satisfaction. Nicole gave him a kiss then rushed off to the shower. Isaiah cut off the TV and called it a night.

A few days had passed since the night of the drunken kiss, and Nicole couldn't seem to keep Jovan out of her head. Something about the way that kiss made her feel had her in a stunned state that she could not shake herself from. She had to be careful not to let his name slip out of her mouth while around Isaiah, which was becoming more and more difficult to do. Friday rolled around again, and Nicole was heading to a lunch date with Kiesha to discuss all that had taken place. As usual, Nicole was running late, so by the time she got there, Kiesha was already seated with a drink in her hand, mindlessly on her phone. "Thought you might have sent me off," she said. Nicole dropped her bags in the chair and let her know that she had some last-minute running around for Isaiah, "My bad." She rolled her eyes then lifted her glass to her lips and returned to her texting. "So what do you plan on doing about this whole Jovan situation? You know it isn't going to just go away. I know it's been on your mind too." Nicole couldn't lie or deny, the fact that she had implanted him in a fantasy while having sex with her man told her all she needed to know. "I can't fuck him. I've worked too hard to keep things okay with Isaiah, and no one-night stand is worth losing all that." Kiesha cracked a smirk, took another sip of her drink, and let out a laugh. "See, I always tell you, that's your problem. You're too damn timid, too unwilling to step out of that comfort zone that man has you caged in. Life is all about risk, and you know damn well it's worth it, or you wouldn't be considering it in the first place." Some of what she said was true. Nicole knew there was no harm in looking in another guy's direction or exchanging in some conversation when out, but this was an entirely different level. Accepting that obviously expensive bracelet and allowing him to kiss her were crossing the line, so why wasn't she more bothered by it?

Maybe it was Kiesha getting into her head, or maybe she was finally admitting to herself that she wanted Jovan. Either way, she had made up her mind. Her thoughts couldn't be clear of him until she found out what was there, if anything. Nicole looked down at her phone then scrolled to Jovan's number. Everything inside of her was screaming this was a bad idea and to leave this man alone. She paused then looked over to Kiesha and opened her mouth. "One date." Another long pause. "He gets one, and that's it. And if I get any type of funny feeling or vibe, then I'm done with him completely and returning the bracelet." Kiesha spit up some of her drink as a look of shock overcame her face. "You're serious?" "I mean, you said it yourself, if I don't do something about this, it's just going to keep floating around in my mind. And I just don't have time for those type of problems." She opened Jovan's number and hit dial, listening as it rang for a few seconds. And then a male voice answered, "Hello?" "Hey."

"What's up? Surprised to be hearing from you."

"Not too much, just out grabbing some food. Wanted to ask you something if you aren't too busy."

"For you, I can make time. What's going on?"

"Well, I know originally I turned you down, but after thinking about it, I realized that was rude. You've always been really sweet to me, and you deserve a chance. So if the offer is still available…"

"Yeah, of course, it is. How's tomorrow at seven?"

"That works fine. Can't wait."

Jovan laughed. "Okay, I'll see you tomorrow then."

"Okay, see you then."

Nicole hung up the phone and sunk down in her chair then reached out for her drink, taking a long sip then signaling the waitress for a refill. "What did I just get myself into?" Kiesha let out an obnoxious laugh, halfway falling out of the chair. "This is going to be hilarious," she said.

Chapter 3

NICOLE HAD NEVER been a very good liar, even when it came to the most minor of white lies. Above all else, she had never legitimately lied to Isaiah. Now she was left with the impossible task of lying straight to his face about where she would be going tonight. Normally, when she had planned to go out for the evening, she would tell him a day prior. That gave him time to catch his attitude, make smart comments, then accept it and move on. This was a different circumstance. Fear was one hell of a motivator that prevented her from saying something until a few hours before the date was set to occur.

With only a couple hours left before Isaiah got off work, she knew she had to think quick. As she went through her closet to look for something to wear, she contemplated on what kind of lie she could say. *Maybe I can tell him I'm going to that new reggae club with a couple friends*, she thought to herself. *No, he would only say he wants to join me.* Nicole picked out something to wear that was not too revealing but still send Jovan a message and something that Isaiah wouldn't disapprove. She pulled out some black leggings from express, which shows off her apple-bottom ass, and a low-cut white shirt. When in doubt, leggings are always a good choice. Nicole threw her clothes on the bed then hopped in the shower. Right there was when the perfect lie hit her. Meanwhile, across town, Isaiah was just about ready to get off work and kick it with the guys. "It's been a while since we all hung out. Let's go down to that new bar," he told his boys. His friend Tremayne shouted, "Aite, that's what's up. I'll meet you there by eight." "All right, cool. Let me get home, shower up and shit, and let the misses know what's going on," Isaiah said while leaving out.

When Isaiah walked into the house, he saw Nicole already dressed for a night out. "Where you headed to, girl?" he asked. "I'm headed to that art gallery they just opened up with a couple of my girlfriends." She knew he would decline that since he thought the only men who went down there were them stuck-up, lame motherfuckers. "Cool. Imma shower up and head to the bar with a couple of the guys." "All right, bae. I'll text you throughout the night," Nicole said as she grabbed her purse. When Nicole got in the car, she realized it was already six thirty. "Ugh, I'm going to be late." Nicole texted Jovan to let him know she on her way to the restaurant. He replied with a smiley face and said he was en route to. As Isaiah hopped out the shower, he realized that Nicole's ass has been out a lot with her friends lately. That was the first sign of suspension.

On the ride to the restaurant, she gave Kiesha a call. "Girl, here goes nothing. I'm headed out to meet him. Hope it goes well," Nicole told Kiesha. "So how did you manage to make it out the house without him asking a million questions?" "Girl, he had plans to go to the bar anyway, so he ain't stress. I can't believe how easy it was." Kiesha laughed. "I told you it will be cool. Let me know how this li'l date goes, girl." Nicole rolled her eyes. "Okay, I'll hit you up a little later." As she parked her car, she threw on some lipstick and a little perfume and put on the diamond bracelet he brought her. Jovan was already at the table with two glasses of wine and was checking his watch. "Hello, gorgeous," Jovan said while pulling out her chair. "Hey, sorry for being so late. Had some stuff to do first," she explained. "Wouldn't be right if you weren't late as usual. You're still the same old Nicole, late for everything but on point when you arrive," he smirked. "That's just how I am. I guess you can say I get it from my mother." "That and a whole lot of other things," Jovan quickly add. "It's been years since we've finally been out on a one-on-one type thing. When you got together with Isaiah, I was kind of pushed to the sideline." Nicole responded with a snappy remark, "Well, he is the man who swept me off my feet.

I mean, somebody had to since you wouldn't." "Yeah, if you say so, but you're sitting here with me right now. So I guess I did something right." She looked down at the menu as if she was thinking of a response. "What's good to eat here? How's the alfredo?" Nicole asked while taking a sip of wine. "That's pretty good. Imma get that too," Jovan said. "You know, I should be the one you marry, not someone who's only in it to control you as his pawn. If you be with me, I'll treat you like a queen. As you can see, I've already started with the bracelet. You're a good girl, a little rough around the edges, but nothing we can't work out," Jovan said as if he could no longer keep it to himself. "Yeah, well, I'm in love with that man, and it's easy to say things when you're on the outside looking in," she replied. "Well, let me in, so I can see the bigger picture," he said as he leaned back in the chair and flagged the waiter over. "Did you guys decide on what you're going to get on this lovely evening." "Yeah, we'll both take the alfredo, and can I have a bottle of wine. I have a feeling were going to be here for a while."

All right, I'll bring the wine over promptly, and the food shall be here shortly," the waiter said. Nicole glazed into his eyes as she wondered what have she gotten herself into. *It's going to be a long night,* she thought. Meanwhile at the bar, Isaiah and his boys started to get tipsy. "Aye, where your girl at, man? She usually blowing up your line by now," Tremayne asks. "Her ass been kicking it with her girls lately. I don't know what's up with that, but I'm not tripping. A lot more free time for me, if you know what I mean." "Good shit, where are the bitches? Finally got my guy back just like them college days!" Tremayne yelled over the music. "Can't be like that. A man like me was too much of player, but umm, ain't nothing wrong with meeting a new friend. Shorty with the braids at the end of the bar keep looking at me. She just might be my first victim." "Man, you ain't shit, boy!" Craig yelled. "What!" "Here you go, your old faithful ass. Fuck you talking about!" Tremayne shouted. "If that's your girl and you love her, why would you put her through that pain like you did before? You lucky she took your black ass back." "Man, fuck are you tripping on? She knows what it is. I love her. She loves me. You act like I'm fucking the bitch. I'm just going to go say what's up," Isaiah said while looking at Craig as if he was tripping. "Yeah, by the end of the night, she be a victim, all right," Craig said while smirking.

Back in the day when Isaiah and Nicole first got together, he was nothing nice. The man couldn't be loyal to save his life. His motto was, until he's married, he's a free man. Nicole, on the other hand, was a goner the first week. She couldn't get enough of him even after finding pictures of naked girls in his phone. It wasn't until he hit rock bottom that he noticed she would be by his side through thick and thin. This man had lost his job, then his condo downtown, and one of his crazy hoes busted the windows out his car. Those were what made him change his ways. When he was out on his luck, Nicole was the one right by his side. Isaiah just couldn't believe he could do her so wrong and she was still by his side. Then his jealous side began to show; he would always accuse her of cheating because he knew there was no way she could be still be faithful. Although there was no evidence, his own guilt weighed a ton on him. Nicole was hurt by it, but she knew that one day, he would come around and be the man she needed. So far, besides controlling ways, it has been going good and worth the time she has put in.

Isaiah made his way to the end of the bar and asked the mysterious woman her name. "My name is Dominique, Nique for short." "Well, Ms. Nique, I saw you looking at me, so I decided to come over and introduce myself. The name's Isaiah." "Well, Mr. Isaiah, how about you have a sit and buy a pretty lady a drink? I'll have another long island," she responded as she flagged down the bartender, signaling for a refill. *Damn, shorty, that's how you get down. I know just how to handle you.* A few drinks later, he found himself in the bathroom fucking the shit out of her without a care in the world. As Isaiah finished up and walked out, Craig looked at him and shook his head as he shouted, "I told you, man! Now that bitch has to take that walk of shame!" "Well, did you get her number?" Treymayne asked. "Hell, naw, for what! Already got the pussy, and ain't no bitch going in my phone for Nicole to see. That shit dead." "Hope you stripped up." Isaiah didn't say anything. He just gave them that look as if he can answer his own questions. Nique walked up and slid her number in his pocket as she walked out the bar. Isaiah passed it over to Treymayne while shouting, "I have no use for it anymore! Had a good night with the hoe! Now let's turn the fuck up!" "Aye, bartender! We need three shots of Henn. Keep them coming!" Craig yelled.

As the fellas drank the night away, Nicole and Jovan headed to the lake front to finish up their conversation. "So are you going to let me show you better?" Jovan asked. "Will it be better or just something different?" He smirked and said it would be all of the above. Nicole cracked a smile then looked off at the lake while digging her feet into the sand as her mind started to drift off into the distance. She stretched out and lay her head back on the blanket Jovan had taken out of his back seat. Looking down, she realized her phone had fallen out of her back pocket. She paused for a second, slowly reaching out to grab it then noticing that she hadn't texted Isaiah all night. *Shit*, she thought. *I know he's pissed I told him I would text him throughout the night, and it's damn near one o'clock.* She started to grab the phone off the ground, and right as her hand was placed around it, Jovan's hand intercepted hers. She looked up with her eyebrow raised, wondering what he was doing. "I just got to see if I missed any calls or anything like that." "You spend every moment with everyone else. The time you have with me is mine, and I'm not sharing." She knew not checking her phone was a bad idea, but she decided that for the moment, it couldn't hurt. She could always tell Isaiah later that her phone died. Jovan reached out to her next, wrapping one of his arms around her waist and pulling her in close to his side. She looked up at the sky and enjoyed the peaceful silence. As she lay there, that curiosity crept back into her mind. *I'm surprised he hasn't tried anything yet. Maybe he's just content with this. So why is a part of me disappointed by that?*

Looking up at him, she saw he wasn't paying much attention either. It seemed as if his mind was wandering just like hers was. *You've waited for what feels like forever to get her alone to yourself, and you're just going to stare at the stars. If you really want her to be yours, you're going to have to show her you can give her something special—not jewelry or a car, something deeper more than what she's getting now. She deserves better. Make her understand that you can be that.* With a split-second decision, she blinked, and he was on top of her. A part of her immediately wanted to fight back and tell him to get off, but she didn't. She knew that she wanted this and had been for a while now. It was something about him and how he touched her that was different. Usually when Isaiah and her had sex, it was all aggression and force; it was what she liked, but this was something else, something more romantic. He wasn't just in this for a thrill; he was putting himself inside of her in another kind of way. He met her lips and sucked on them softly then pulled away slowly, nibbling on her bottom lip and tracing it with his tongue. He began running his hands up her blouse and unhooking her bra while running his mouth down to her neck. He dug his teeth into her skin, gnawing until he saw it was leaving marks, then moved to another spot and started over again. Knowing that her neck had always been a weak spot for her, Nicole couldn't help but let out a moan and pull Jovan in closer.

She started unbuckling his pants, pulling them down as low as possible with him still on top of her. Her thong was already soaked, and she could feel how hard his dick was through his boxers. He climbed up higher onto her as she reached her hand out and started stroking his dick from the outside of his boxers, then pulling them down, she wrapped her legs around his waist. He was already hard as a rock, and she could feel him throbbing in her hand and didn't want to wait any longer. Just as she was about to shove his dick into her, she felt him sliding down her stomach. He pulled down her leggings then yanked her thong off from around her waist. Outing her clit with his tongue was making her twitch in his arms as she was trying her best to brace herself for the head she felt approaching. She had experienced good head before, even great, but she was not at all prepared for the sensation he sent through her body the moment his tongue entered her. He was rolling and vibrating in each and every direction he could find. You would think it was battery operated by the speed and rotation he was able to manifest. *This was not head; no man can do this,* Nicole thought to herself. She had to keep forcing her eyes back open and looking down to convince herself this was him, not a vibrator. His back was already red from the imprint of her hands and nails tearing away as if that was the only outlet she had for what she was feeling. Arching her back, she felt a sharp chill ran up her spine as she gripped the back of his head and felt herself cum down his tongue. Eyes rolling back and legs shaking, her head fell back as she collapsed, only to be brought right back up by the penetrating feeling of his dick entering her drenched lips. He was slowly stroking her at first, digging in deep then pulling out to rub around the outside of her clit then grinding back inside her. Left side, right side in, and back out, his dick was exploring every aspect of her pussy, and it was driving her up a fucking wall. Each time she thought the spot he was hitting was heaven and couldn't get any better, he would slide back in and find a new area, causing an even better feeling. His dick was already shining from all the juice it was collecting from her pussy. She pushed him off for a moment to clean his tool off with her lips and catch a taste then stuck it back inside of her. She pushed him out again then bent over positioning her ass up in the air spreading her legs wide open. It didn't take two seconds before his hands were gripped at her side and his dick was right back inside of her. Her head went straight into the ground from the shock of feeling like he slipped into her stomach. With nothing to grab but the sand, she cracked her nails banging at the ground and screaming at the top of her lungs. His right hands cocked back and smacked her ass, making her neck jerk over and over again. She loved being dominated like this. Her neck swung to the left, and she threw her head back to look at all the work Jovan was putting in on her pussy. "That's right, fuck. Show me you deserve this shit! Show me you can do me better!" It didn't take her to say it for him to take that hint. Jovan was grinding his hips into her, giving her every inch he had like there was something on the line to prove.

Wrapping her hand around the back of her neck, he sped up his strokes, pinning her to the ground as he went in faster with each passing second. Panting, he pulled his dick almost entirely out before shoving it back inside and repeating this process as he felt her lips grip the outside of his dick, almost as if it was fighting to keep him inside. He could feel the pressure building up inside of him and knew he couldn't hold his nut much longer, so Jovan flipped Nicole on her back then picked up both legs and pulled them on his shoulders. Thrusting his dick inside of her, he could feel his head hitting the farthest wall. Nicole clenched up, wrapping her thighs around his neck and dragging him down until he was only a few inches away from her face. He looked down, trying to keep her still as she shook uncontrollably under him. Nicole lunged at his neck biting with all the force her jaws could muster and screamed into him as she lost her grip, pushing him off and climaxing right before her body collapsed. It was at that very moment Jovan lost it as well and shot his load onto her then fell back onto the sand. The two lay there without saying a word—with sweat dripping off both their bodies, heavily breathing, and with both their eyes closing.

Chapter 4

THE SMELL OF something cooking in the kitchen awoke Nicole from a deep sleep. She got out of bed, slipped on her house shoes, and walked toward the kitchen. As she got closer, she heard "Stand by Me" by Ben E. King playing on the radio. She thought to herself, *What is he up to this morning?* "Good morning," Isaiah said as he kissed her on the lips and pulled out her chair. "What's going on in here? This is unusual." "Just felt like doing something special for you this morning and make you breakfast since, umm, you can't cook," he said with a smirk. "For your information, I can get down on some breakfast food. That's my specialty," she snapped back. "Well, today just sit back and enjoy your pancakes, bacon, sausage and drink your orange juice." "Well, I thank you, bae." "No problem," Isaiah said as he took his seat across from her. Since the night of the cheating scandal on both parties, no one brought it up. Both were filled with guilt and figured it wouldn't be wise to accuse the other for the exact thing they did. "This week has started off exceptionally well for the both of us, and it's Friday. We both off for the weekend, what should we do?" Nicole asked him as she stuffed pancakes in her mouth. "I don't know, it's a nice day. Maybe a picnic in the park?" "Well, actually, that doesn't sound too bad. I'll pack us lunch after I get out the shower, she responded.

On occasions, Isaiah expressed his love for her; like any man in a relationship, he wanted to treat his lady to a good time. Sex was one thing, but to show her that she was worth more than that was even better. After showers and cleaning, they finally made their way to the park. He put a blanket on the ground for them, and she got the lunches out the box. Every time Nicole looked at him, she wanted to confess, but she knew it was a risk she will be taking. She thought about Jovan at least twice a day. The night at the lake kept replaying over and over in her head. *Could this mean that I don't have to deal with his jealous bullshit and there might be something better out here for me?* she thought to herself. But at the same time, when he did things like this, she felt the little butterflies in her stomach as if they were on their first date again. After about five minutes of soaking up the sun and looking at the view, Isaiah broke the silence. "I know we're both still kind of young, but I know I'll spend the rest of my life with you. When should we have kids? "Kids!" She looked at him as if he was joking. "Yeah, I mean, we're in our early twenties, but I've been thinking about a little boy running around the crib." "Well, that would be nice, but first, we have to get a house, better jobs and fix the problems in our relationship. Aw yeah, how can I forget, I need a ring," she responded. "Okay, you have a point. We do have to iron out of a couple things, but it just's been on my mind." "In due time, honey. Never rush into such a big decision, my mother always said." "Understandable, he said as he cleaned up the mess and shook the crumbs off the cover so he could fold it up. "Looks like rain might be coming. Let's head out, find something indoors to do," he suggested.

As they headed home, he chose to take a different route. He pulled up to a house. In Nicole's suspension, she looked puzzled and asked who stayed there. He pulled out two sets of keys and handed them to her and said, "We do." "What! You got us a fucking house!" Nicole shouted in shock. "Yes, I did. That's one thing off the list of requests you've provided. We're getting closer and closer to our children," Isaiah said with a smile. Nicole hit him in the arm and ran to the house. When she opened the door, she saw that it was fully furnished. "How did you do this?" "I've been secretly saving over time, and the picnic was just a way to get you out the house so we could get the remaining things out the apartment." "Who helped you?" Nicole asked._"The guys came over and moved it out as soon as we left, and the rest of the stuff was just placed like a week ago." "I can't fucking believe this!" she said as she jumped in his arms and kissed him. "I'm trying to prove to you that I can change and become a better man to you. We have our problems, but I'm working on it. This is everything, you know. I've been dying to get out of that nasty apartment. Money will be tight for a couple of months, but we can make it still." "I picked a fucked-up time to cheat on him. Now I don't know what I want," Nicole said to herself while checking out the house. "Well, tonight, let's have a couple people over to show off the house, bae!" she yelled from the kitchen. "That can work. I'll grab a couple of drinks and a little food. Will head to the store now."

Nicole couldn't wait to call Keisha and let her know. "Hello?" Keisha said.

"Girl, guess what!" "What?" "Girl, Isaiah bought me a house!" Nicole shouted. "What the hell, then hit him over the head." "I don't know, but I love it. And we're having a little kickback tonight, so you have to come through." "Hell yeah, I'll be there, girl. I'm thirsty to see what it looks like. Oh, by the way, you never told me about your little date with you-know-who!" Keisha shouted as if she was anxious to hear the details. "Just know that it was one to remember," she responded. "Holding out on the goods, I see. You know you want to tell me." In a low voice, Nicole told her the details about the sex. "What!" Keisha yelled. "I knew it, I knew it," she laughed. "Don't judge me, girl. I couldn't help it, and now he's been on my mind heavy." "Well, that's one secret that you definitely should not tell Isaiah. I know you don't do good with things like this, but it will ruin your relationship. Maybe a little space between you and Jovan would do you some good." "I've been ignoring his calls and deleting text messages all week." "Good. Remember who's number 1. And in due time, you will be able to contact him, but this is too fresh," Keisha said. "Yeah, you're right," Nicole said then she ended the conversation. Nicole began to make herself at home but still in disbelief. She flopped on the couch and turned on the TV until Isaiah got back. After about an hour he comes in with the groceries and put them up. As he made his way over to the couch, she started to take off his shirt and said, "Before the company, we should bless our new house." "Damn, bae, that's why I love your ass," he said as he dropped his pants. She attacked him as if she hasn't had sex in over a year. He was surprised by her actions but enjoyed the new moves she was putting on him. Nicole completely took charge of the sex. Partially because this was the first time she had sex with him since her and Jovan's steamy intercourse, and besides, she was extremely sexually frustrated. From scratching up his back to biting his lips, it forced him to bust a little earlier than normal. She flipped over and sat on the couch next to him, breathing hard. Isaiah looked at her and wiped the sweat from her forehead. "If not giving you nothing in only a week gets me this, imagine what a month will get me." She smiled and gestured for him to head toward the shower for round 2. He didn't think twice as he jumped up and followed her to the master bathroom. Isaiah grabbed her arms and choked her just enough to her satisfaction and looked her in the eyes as he told her softly but firmly "I'm in charge this round" while he slowly stroked her, teasing her knowing she wanted it fast and hard. He bit on her neck and sucked on her nipples then turned her around and bent her over. As he placed both hands on her breasts, he powerdrive her until he exploded on her back. She stood up and kissed him then washed up and headed to the room to get dressed. He stayed in the shower trying to wrap his head around what just happened, as if it was so fast his thoughts weren't able to catch up with his actions.

A few weeks have passed since the night at the beach with Jovan and Nicole. She has been sticking to her approach of avoiding him at all cost. Even when she would reply to texts, she would be very brief and very reserved, doing all she could to avoid speaking about that night—a plan that seemed to be working all too well until one faithful afternoon when that all fell apart. Nicole was wrapping up a workout session at the gym. While heading back to her car, she saw Jovan getting out of his car. *Shit!* she thought to herself. *When did he start coming here?* She hoped she could get past him without him realizing it was her, but it took all of two seconds for him to recognize her and proceed to walk over.

"Well, look who it is. Where have you been hiding, stranger?" She looked down at her feet awkwardly, as a sinking feeling overtook her stomach, and she forced herself to make eye contact. "Hey... Uh, how you been?" He put a sarcastic smirk on his face. "Well, aside from you dodging me these last few weeks, I've been fine. What about you?" "I… uh… I've been decent, just busy. You know how it is." She felt like shit for disrespecting Jovan and treating him poorly—having sex with him then barely speaking to him afterwards, treating him like a cheap one-night stand. She knew that he did not deserve that at all. Whether he deserved it or not, she knew she couldn't risk her relationship with Isaiah for him. Looking up, she saw his facial expression change from jokingly to serious and irritated. "Right, yeah, I know how it is, Nicole. Look, we aren't some kids in college where you sleep with me then try looking past me when we see each other. We are adults. If you weren't feeling it afterwards, that's all you had to say. So don't hit me with that excuse." He was angry and had every right to be for what she had done. She started to open her mouth to respond, but she wasn't sure where to begin. An "I'm sorry" wouldn't do it justice, and saying it was a mistake would just be more insulting than not speaking to him all this time. "I know I was childish for how I went about things, but you have to see where I'm coming from. All problems aside, I love my man and he makes me happy, and that night with you was just something that caught me off guard." As she started to continue, he cut her off. "Look, Nicole, you can say what you want, but I'm not buying it. You had to have felt something that night, just like I did. If it really was just sex, you would've been able to say that from the start and move on with your life. The fact that you worked so hard to avoid me for all this time shows me you were nervous and afraid because you knew something was there. If you really want to put it behind you, then I'll respect that, but you have to do one thing for me first." She didn't speak right away because she knew everything he was saying was the truth. "Okay… What's the one thing?" she asked. He showed a sign of relief that she had accepted his condition, instead of just shooting him down and walking to the car.

Jovan grabbed her hand and asked her to have dinner with him one last time. He figured it was his last chance. And if after this last time if she feels the same way, then he would leave and would never bring it up again. "I want to really sit and talk and really speak about how I feel and your feelings toward me. I'm not with leaving things unsaid, if this is really about to be the end of our story." Now something deep inside her was screaming to say no and tell him she couldn't do this any longer, but it just wouldn't come out. "Fine, just this one dinner, and then that's it." Jovan nodded his head and then walked a little closer to give her a hug and sneak a kiss before walking to the gym. Her first instinct was to look around the parking lot, hoping nobody had seen any of what had just taken place. Luckily, the parking lot was empty. She let out a sigh of relief and walked to her car, packing in her gym bag and pulling off. Unfortunately for her, the parking lot was not as empty as she thought. Isaiah's friend Treymayne had been sitting in his truck across from her and had seen everything that just happened. Without even knowing, she had just fucked up majorly and would soon see how much.

Isaiah was leaving the store when he stopped in midstep to the sound of his phone vibrating in his pocket. He walked to the car then opened up the door while reaching to answer it. "Yeah, what's up, bro?" "Not shit, man, you're busy?" Isaiah proceeded to load the groceries in the car while juggling his phone. "Nah, well, not really. What's going on?" Treymayne asked if he was sitting down before delivering the news. "Well, I got something to tell you, and I'm not sure how you're going to handle it. It's not an easy pill to swallow." After he finished loading in everything, he started the engine and responded, "Sounds like something serious, so just come out and say it. Don't sugarcoat it." He took a deep breath then proceeded to talk. "Look, man, I was heading to the gym, and when I was about to get out of my truck, I saw Nikki." "Okay? And?" "And she was with some guy, and it looked like they were talking about some serious shit. Before dude walked away, he kissed her." The phone went silent for a moment. "Are you fucking kidding me! Are you positive it was her? I need to know before I snap and catch a fucking case!" "Yeah, man, I'm sure it was her. No doubt in my mind about that. I wouldn't even call you on a maybe. Look, I heard them saying something about a conversation they had over dinner. That's all I could make out. Just wanted to let you know, but I got to go. I'll hit you up later. Don't do anything off the wall, man. Try to keep a level head." Isaiah hung up the phone then sat in silence for a minute before punching the steering wheel then pulling off.

I can't believe this shit. After all these years, all this time, and she's the one getting caught up. I mean, damn, I know I wasn't the best guy, but shit, I was supposed to be the screwup, not her. This shit is not going to fly. As he drove back home with a million thoughts racing through his mind, he continued asking himself how was he going to go about handling this situation. He knew one thing for sure: before this day was over, this was going to get resolved, and he was going to get all the answers about this situation and this mystery guy.

Chapter 5

SHIT AROUND HERE *will never be the same*, Isaiah thought to himself. *This motherfucker just right in the open with the shit. She doesn't give a fuck who's watching.* He sat and tried to figure out exactly how to handle the situation. In this case, two things could happen. One, he could go in the crib and raise hell, curse her out, then throw her shit the fuck out of his house; or two, he could go home, let her know that her secret is out, and they could talk like grown-ups. "This girl here is not supposed to be doing this shit, but who am I to judge." A thousand things ran across his mind for what felt like the longest drive ever, but in reality, the house was only fifteen minutes away. Before he walked into the house, Isaiah gathered his emotions and walked in with a mad but curious look on his face. He went into the living room then the bedroom then bathroom, but there was no Nicole. Isaiah sat in the dark until she got home. As soon as she walked in the house, he jumped up and began to question her. "Who the fuck is this man you kissing on and going out with, Nicole!" She looked puzzled trying to figure out where to start and wondering how he found out. Nicole began to plead for him to calm down and just take a seat. "Hell, naw! Tell me now. I'm running around buying houses and shit, and you doing dicks!" Nicole begged for him to sit down so she could tell him what happened. He took a sit, but she could see fumes coming out of his head.

"There's no other way to start than by saying sorry and I never meant to hurt you," Nicole said with tears in her eyes. "I love you, and no one will ever take that away. It was a mistake that should have never happened. That night, I just needed to see what being with someone else would be like. He treated me different, and it felt good. I was vulnerable, and he just happened to be there at that time. Ever since that night, I've been beating myself up, and I wanted to tell you—believe me, I did—but then, we got the house. I spoke to Keisha, and I just couldn't do it. I felt like shit for these last weeks knowing what I have done to you. Over the years, you have fucking hurt me time after time, and for once, I needed to just let my hair down and relax. I'm not saying that I should've taken that route, but it happened, and I'm so sorry. I didn't want to lose you." At this point, Isaiah was trying to find out the right words to say. The only thing he wanted to do was just beat her ass. "Maybe you aren't the person who I thought you were. You aren't nothing but a lying-ass cheater, and I don't want to wife no hoe." Nicole yelled out, "It was one fucking time! I haven't cheated on you any other time since we've been together."

Men can be funny at times. As long as they're the ones cheating, it's okay, but as soon as their girl ventures to other things, she's not worth nothing to them. "You're walking around here with your chest poking out like you've been faithful to me since day 1. Remember, I'm the one that held you down when the crazy-ass bitches made you lose your job or busted the windows out your car. Now I fuck up once, and I'm the hoe," she snapped back. "Maybe shit between us isn't as healthy as I thought it was. I've left my cheating ways in the past. Yeah, I slipped up here and there, but I never thought you would do that shit," he responded. "I get it now. You're going to beat me up over this forever and hold this shit over my head. There is nothing that I can do to prove to you it will never happen again. To be honest, Jovan showed me that I don't have to deal with your bullshit anymore, so I'm going to pack some clothes up and stay over Keisha's house for a day or two to let you cool down. Maybe some time apart will do us justice," Nicole said. "You know what, you let that punk-ass man get in your head and fill it up with a bunch of shit, and now you're going to come to me and try to tell me about my bullshit and what it put you through. Let's not forget you're the one that just got caught cheating, and it's no way around that. You not about to come in and make me feel like I'm the bad guy. So you want to pack a bag? Get enough for your ass to stay gone. I don't need this fucking shit. I should beat the shit out of you. Hurry the fuck up and get out!" he shouted. "You're right. Just don't blow my damn phone up like you always do when I walk out this door," she snapped back and rolled her eyes. Isaiah didn't respond. He just kept looking at SportsCenter and then grabbed a beer. Nicole grabbed some stuff and slammed the door then called up Keisha and let her know she was on her way.

As she pulled off, she started to think about actually leaving him for good, what would she gain and what will she lose, and is the grass really greener on the other side. Nicole pulled up at Keisha's house with her makeup all messed up from crying in the car. Keisha opened the door and asked what happened as she gave her a hug. "He found out that I cheated and told me to get my shit and get out." "What! How did he find out, who told him, and when did this happen?" Kiesha was so confused she didn't know what to ask first. "I don't know who told him. All I know is that I ran into Jovan at the gym and agreed to meet with him just one more time. He then hugged me and kissed me, that's all. Then I left." "You don't think Jovan told him, do you?" "Naw, I doubt that. He's not that type of guy—he wouldn't do that to me," Nicole said. "Well, somebody must have seen you guys in the parking lot or something." "I looked around, and I didn't see anyone. I'm just so overwhelmed right now I just need to sleep. I don't know what I want to do at this point." "Well, your room is already for you, and I'll be out here if you can't sleep," Keisha told her. Nicole thanked her then headed to the cabinets to grab a couple glasses and a bottle of wine. She figured maybe that will help her sleep. With no thought about, Keisha pulled up a chair, and they began to figure out what was the next step. Nicole pondered if she should text Jovan and let him know what just went down. Keisha told her that maybe it was not so bad to let him know. "Just stick to the basic. Don't give him anymore lead way than needed." Nicole agreed that she would go ahead and tell him, but in the morning after she has had time to sleep on it.

The following days seemed to drag by with the same set of patterns. Nicole would wake up doing random things around the house to keep her mind off everything that was going on, periodically stopping to check her phone for a message or call while contemplating if she should send one of her own to either one of the men. Her conscience told her it would be for the best to continue waiting all this out until she had decided on her next path of action. She didn't even realize among all the deep thinking that she had ran low on clothes as well as her other supplies when she had rushed out the house after the argument with Isaiah. She thought about the best way to go about getting a few more of her things from the house, but she knew for a fact that she wasn't prepared to face him yet. While sitting on the couch with legs stretched out across the table, she heard the sound of the key turning in the knob, and it slowly opened to reveal Keisha standing there. She looked like she had just finished going for a run and still had her running attire on—some tight spandex-looking shorts along with a sports bra covered by a purple Nike tank top and her hair tied in a ponytail.

"Well, somebody is up early, I see. You couldn't make some food since you wanted to be an early bird, huh?" Nicole couldn't help but let out a laugh at her friend's cleat joke, considering she knew that she couldn't cook to save her life. "Ha ha, very funny. Nah, I'm just up doing some thinking, you know. I haven't really been able to sleep in like I wanted to lately. That and I am almost out of clothes." Keisha had walked into the kitchen and was finishing off a bottle of water and about to take off her shoes when she finally realized what Nicole was saying. She let out a sigh and stopped unlacing her shoes. "Do you want me to go by the house and get you a few more of your things? I already needed to go that way and stop by the store, so it wouldn't be a problem. You don't seem to ready to see Isaiah yet anyway."

Nicole stopped to think it over, and the idea didn't sound like a bad one, to be honest. She did need some more of her things, and like she said, she was already going in that direction. She began rummaging through her bag looking for her set of keys to the house. She had just been playing with them the previous night, envisioning the moment when she could confidently walk back into her home without worrying about the situation any longer. After looking a bit longer, she found the keys then proceeded to walk them over to Keisha. "I just need a few more shirts and some bottoms, and if you see it sitting out, grab my laptop. If not, then don't worry about it I don't want you having to look for it then bumping into Isaiah." Keisha took the keys then let out a sarcastic snicker. "Girl, nobody worried about running into that man, but don't worry, I'll get your stuff. But while I'm gone, order us some food. I'm starving and don't feel like cooking today." "Fine, I'll take care of the food crises you're having, and thank you." Keisha headed to the door while grabbing her car keys and her purse then turned around and whispered, "Hmm, if I get back here with all your stuff and don't see any food, it's going to be a where-you-living crises going on in here." Nicole burst out into laughter at her friend's rude joke. "I can't stand your ass." Keisha closed the door behind her.

She hopped in her car and pulled out of the driveway deciding she would go to the house and get Nicole her things first because it shouldn't take that long. It took all of twenty minutes to arrive; traffic was very light or the fact that it was still very early. She walked up the sidewalk to the front step and walked into the house. It was dead silent, as if no one had been home in a few days, though there was no mess to be seen. Keisha walked upstairs to the bedroom she knew to be theirs and started rummaging through the closet and drawers for what Nicole had requested her to bring back. After loading a small bag, she looked around for the computer, when she heard what sounded like a back door being opened downstairs. She decided she would leave the computer and come back at another time and headed down the hallway and back downstairs. Upon reaching the bottom of the staircase, she saw Isaiah sitting there, eating at the kitchen table with a puzzled look on his face. For a moment, she thought he would just stare without saying a word as she left, but right as she reached out to grab the knob of the front door, she heard him start to speak. "Would you mind telling me what the hell you are doing in my house?" It wasn't a harsh way that he said it, but there was clearly a sense of irritation in his voice as he turned his body at the table to face the door. She waited a moment before releasing the knob and turning to face him. "Look, I just came by to get some of her stuff. No drama needed. I got what she needed, so now, I'm going to leave." She turned around and headed for the door again, but he interrupted her once again. "You know, this shit is really your fault." Her body switched around in the blink of an eye. "Excuse me, my fault?" she responded with an attitude on her face. "Yeah, I didn't stutter—your damn fault. She was different before you came around. She wasn't so eager to go out at every chance and didn't drink like that. You've been a negative influence since she met you." The look of shock on Keisha's face was beyond her belief; the words she was hearing she could not believe. "Are you serious right now? You treat her like shit and cheat on her for years, and you sit there with a straight face and blame me for this?" Again, Keisha was in shock from the fact that Isaiah was sitting there trying to blame her for Nicole's actions and doing it with a straight face. It was in that moment he stood up from the table and walked over to her until he was about three feet away then stopped. Isaiah then told her that the only way he has been able to stay calm and levelheaded was the fact that Nicole was talked into doing something this bogus. "I know I wasn't the best man in the world, but she understood. She was patient with me and knew I was trying to do better. Then you come around filling her head with bullshit and dragging her around all these dudes. It was only a matter of time."

Keisha was furious at the fact that he was seriously sitting there wanting to put it all on her. Her body felt like it was on fire. Never before had she heard of a man trying to justify something like this, and she didn't know what to say. "Let me tell you something. You have to be quite possibly the weakest-minded man I have ever come across in my life. You have a perfectly good woman at home, and you choose to run the streets like a little-ass boy because you aren't ready to grow up and be a man. Then the day finally comes, and your good woman gets tired of your bullshit and goes out and finds a man ready to step up and be what she needs. You sit here seeing all this, and instead of seeing your fault and wanting to improve to make her happy, you choose to place the blame on one of her friends. Does that really make any sense to you?" Isaiah paused then took another step forward. "See, that right there is my point. That "step up and be what she needs" bullshit, that's the little lines you've been feeding her." This time, Keisha took a step forward in his direction, trying her best to keep her composure. "She doesn't need your shit in her life anymore. She wants future without drama, and clearly yours isn't mature enough to give that to her yet. You only bought this house to blind her from more of your mistakes that you had coming. It's just what you do. You know you don't want that settled-down lifestyle yet, but you keep pulling her back in because you don't want anyone else to have her. All you do is bait her with shit you know she wants. Next it will be a baby, followed by more of your fuckups. If you want to put this on me, go ahead, I'll take the blame for opening her eyes to a life other than the one you've led her to believe is her only option." Keisha didn't realize it, but now they were both standing directly in front of each other. No more than a few inches separated the two. "Clearly you're the expert on the subject. It slipped my mind you were notorious for your long, happy relationships." Isaiah smirked after his comment, looking down at her with his arms folded as if he was waiting on her to respond with a comeback. "If I'm such a waste of time and space, why are you still here speaking with me?"

Keisha opened her mouth to say something, but no words left from her lips. She didn't really have an answer to that. Why hadn't she left yet? For that matter, why was she so close to him? Her body was not responding the way she thought it would, and a strangeness had overtaken her because, for some unknown reason, she was getting turned on by this situation. The animosity, the anger, the overall loathing she had always had for Isaiah was manifesting itself, but not in the way that she thought it would. It was like every fiber of her being was telling her to attack him and released all this tension that had been building for so long but through sex.

As they stood face-to-face, Keisha reached in and leaned for a kiss, one that she has been wanting deep down inside.

Isaiah grabbed her hair, tilted her head to the side, then put her on the kitchen counter. She began to unbutton his jeans while he sucked on her neck. In the midst of their foreplay, Keisha butt-dialed Nicole. "Hello! Hello!" Nicole shouts through the phone. The only thing she can hear on the other side are moans and groans. In disbelief of what she heard, she called Isaiah's phone but no answer, then tried Keisha's phone again but got the same results. While Nicole was at home going crazy and wondering what her next move was going to be, Isaiah and Keisha were having other plans going on. As Isaiah took off her jeans, he began to give her head. She moaned and screamed as if she was trying to get away, but the tight grip he had of her had limited her space. When he came back up, she stopped him and brought up Nicole, as if the damage wasn't already done. Isaiah said, "Fuck that shit," and began to put his dick inside and hit her with rough, fast stokes. She closed her eyes and leaned back on the counter and let him take over. He flipped her over and fucked her from the back while he palmed her ass then exploded on her backside. Keisha jumped down and grabbed her phone to check and see who has been blowing up her phone, then she realized that she called Nicole by accident. She looked up at Isaiah and shook her head as if she was ashamed.

Chapter 6

FURIOUS AT WHAT she heard a while ago, Nicole didn't even know what to do. She started to pack up what little she had at her ex-best friend's house and called up Chantelle for a much-needed vent session. "Girl, you would never guess what's been going on in my hectic life," Nicole said. "Girl, it seems like I haven't seen you since the birthday party." "Well, me and Keisha are no longer friends, and I'm no longer with Isaiah!" "OMG! What happened? I can't believe you and Keisha aren't fucking with each other," Chantelle said. Nicole began to explain what happened and how she had overheard the two of them fucking and all the events that led up to the breakup between her and

Isaiah. After talking for a while, they decided to set up a time to go and chat it up over some drinks. Chantelle agreed and then ended the call.

Without calling or anything, Nicole just showed up at Jovan's door. Luckily for her, he was home. As he opened the door, he can tell that she has been through hell and back. He reached out for a hug then grabbed her suitcase as they walked in the house. Nicole began to explain everything that happened and let him know what Keisha has done. "So let me get this straight. His 'friend' sees us kiss, and he kicks you out? That's crazy, that man been the biggest cheater I know," Jovan said. "Yeah, I lost my man and my best friend within a two-week span." "Everything happens for a reason. Who knows how long this thing between the two of them have been going on," Jovan said as he handed her a water bottle. As Nicole began to look upset at the fact that things will never be the same and that she has lost her best friend, Jovan tried his best to lift her spirits just a little. "You've lost Kiesha, which I can see is devastating, but Isaiah was worth the loss. He doesn't let you shine and finds a way to keep you tied down on a short leash." "He cheats on me with so many other women, and the one time I do it, I'm a hoe and aren't worth shit," Nicole said as she wiped her tears and collapsed into the couch and buried her head into Jovan's chest.

Nicole has done everything for that man down to an absolute T. There was nothing he could have asked for, nothing that he could desire that she would not do or find a way to make it happen. Through all the heartbreak, all the lies and fake smiles, she stayed by his side to end up here. It just didn't make sense to Nicole. Jovan pulled her closer into him and ran his hand through her hair, looking down at her and wondering how everything had all gone so badly. "I'm sorry, not just for this but everything that has happened. It all feels like it's me to blame for your stress and sorrows." She wiped her face on his shirt then pulled herself up just enough to make eye contact. "That's not true. Please don't look at it that way. You're the only one that ever cared enough to try to give me something better." "Well, even so. It isn't right for him to do this to you then turn around and make you feel like shit for it. He didn't deserve you from the start, and everything else leading up to this point has been evidence of that." Nicole let out a long sigh then slowly lowered her face back into his chest, and there was silence for a while. "So what is it that you want to do now? I mean, now that everything is out in the open," Jovan asked. She wasn't sure what to say. The man who had been by her side for as long as she could remember was gone, and the friend who felt like a sister and her safe haven was also gone. Feeling as if she lost her right and left hand confused her to no end. Jovan looked down as he felt her grip into his shirt as tight as she could.

"I want them to feel the hurt that I am feeling at this moment. I was a great friend and an amazing girlfriend, and I got forgotten just as easily. And I want them to pay for it." A puzzled look crept across Jovan's face, and for a moment, he wasn't sure what to respond with. "So… Uh, what exactly are you suggesting?" Nicole looked up again, this time pulling herself completely up and moving so she was looking him directly in the eyes. "Do you love me?" she asked. Without any hesitation, he replied, "Yes, of course, I do." "Would you be willing to do something with me to help me move forward with my life, something I feel I need right now even if it's on the extreme side?" "Yes, anything. So tell me what it is you want to do," Jovan said. The room was filled with a silence that could only be compared to death. The breathing of the two people could not even be heard, and in the next instant, she spoke, "Jovan, I want you to help me kill them both!" The look of shock that overcame his face is exactly what Nicole expected, but he did not respond with any sign that she was joking with what she had said to him. "You can't be serious right now." "I've never been more serious at any moment in my life. I am asking you to do this with me. And after that, we leave this town, this city, and we start a new life together, away from all the bullshit that's been causing me hurt all these years. Doesn't matter where we go or what we end up doing, but I cannot move forward in my life until this is done, and I know in my heart that it's true. Sometimes love is taking a gamble on something crazy because it just feels like it's what needed to be done. So yes, this is what I am asking of you."

Another deep sigh filled the air this time; however, it came from Jovan. He has seriously just been asked to commit a murder, to actually take a life, by the woman he loved. There wasn't anything on this earth that could prepare you to respond to something like this. "Since the day I met you, something deep inside of me told me that I was the man that could bring you true happiness on a level that no other person could. I was willing to do whatever it took, if it meant bringing you that happiness that I knew you deserved. If you honestly feel that this is what you need, not just for us but for yourself to be where you need to be, then I'll do it for you," he responded then gave her a kiss and a big hug. "Jovan, we cannot go into this with any type of uncertainty. You have to be on board with me 100 percent." "Yeah, I know, and I am. I will help you kill the both of them, and then we will leave this life behind and go find our new one together."

Chapter 7

WHILE JOVAN AND Nicole got everything they needed together, Isaiah was having trouble of his own. Believe it or not, he took the breakup just as hard. He began to drink heavily and spend all his money at strip clubs with his boys. The thought of the person you planned to live your life with, have kids with, and marry has left for good was weighing heavy on his mind. *What's my next step?* he thought to himself. Now that Isaiah has had sex with Keisha and Nicole found out, he knew there was no chance of ever getting back together. The only thing for Isaiah to do now was to suck it up, remember why he chose to kick her out, and get back to his playboy ways. After he hopped out the shower with the towel around his waist, he looked into the mirror and smiled. "What I'm tripping for, I still got it," Isaiah said to himself with a smirk. After getting dressed, he headed down to the nightclub to meet up with the guys and blow a little steam.

"What's up, homie, how's things going?" Tremayne asked as the rest of them looked up, waiting on Isaiah to respond. "It's been going okay. She's been on my mind heavy, but I know that it's nothing for me but to slip back into my old ways and bring a couple chicks home tonight." The guys all encouraged it with another round of shots to get the party going. While Isaiah drank the night away, Jovan was able to get his hands on a small bottle of poison. He looked at Nicole and let her know it was time to put the plan in motion. Nicole and Jovan thought long and hard, day and night on how they will get away with the murders of two people. Jovan thought long and hard until he reached a logical decision, one that he was sure would work. He looked at Nicole and asked, "What if we kill Isaiah and frame Keisha? She'll go to jail for the murder, he will be dead, and no one will suspect it was you." Nicole looked off into space as if she could picture the future. "I think that can work," she said. "Even though I hate the man, I don't want to torture the man, so I'm guessing the poison is the best solution," Jovan said. "That can work, but how do we involve Kiesha in the mix?" "Well, this is where the plan comes in. Remember that day you gave her your key to the house so she could get some clothes for you?" "Yeah, but what does that have to do with anything?"

Nicole asked. "Well, she still has your key. We can plant the bottle of poison at her house then sneak over to Isaiah's house and use the needle to inject the poison into his drink." "Okay, I can see where you're going with this," Nicole said with a sneaky grin on her face. Jovan continued to speak. "We'll leave a little drop or so somewhere in the kitchen so when they investigate, they will know someone that has recently been in the house put it there. We will have to spark an argument between the two of them, which will give the police a lead that she could've had motive to kill him." "That's unbelievable! That can actually work!" she yelled. "All it will take is a little effort, but we are short on time. If we are going to make this work, it has to be before the week is out." Now, getting people to believe that Isaiah and Keisha hated each other wouldn't be a problem since both have voiced that to their friends on previous occasions.

Nicole sat on the couch with her eyes drifting around the room, rattling her brain on how exactly she could ignite an argument between her former best friend and her lover. She saw flashbacks of the screen replaying in the back of her head. "It has to be something drastic, something that would piss her off so much she wouldn't know what to do with herself. Do you have any ideas?" Jovan remained silent for a moment, but an idea was clearly forming inside of his mind. "Well, from what I can tell of Isaiah and his immaturity after all this took place, I would imagine he's going to go back to his old sleeping ways. So what if we made Isaiah think he got Keisha pregnant? Knowing him, he won't want anything to do with it or with her after losing you. He'd cut her off or start ignoring her, and she'd be so angry and unable to hide it. I think it could work. What do you think?" A mischievous grin overtook Nicole's face, implying that she loved the idea. "That's perfect! He won't even entertain the idea of having a baby with her. I'm sure right now he wants nothing more than to run these streets to try and forget everything that's happened. If he even slightly thinks it's possible, he won't speak to her, and that'll drive her crazy enough to give her an alibi." Jovan reached over to Nicole and pulled her close to him while wrapping both of his arms around her.

"So we have a full plan now aside from one more important thing," Jovan mumbled. Nicole paused and looked up at him. "What important thing is that?" Jovan looked, slighted his head down, and said, "We need to start planning where we are going to go once all this goes down. Granted our plan does sound like it should work without a hitch, it's always a good idea to have a backup plan in case things don't pan out how we want. Leave the state, hell, maybe even the country, but we don't need to be here once the dust starts settling. Is there anywhere you ever wanted to go to live? Because now would be the time to plan for that move." The more he said, the more Nicole realized he was right. Smoothly or not, when their plan started to come about, it would be better for both of their cases if they weren't around to see any bodies drop or possibly have it traced back to either of them. A move, and a far one at that, was necessary. "You know, I've always wanted to live in Cali—somewhere lively with a lot of people and beautiful weather, plenty of things to entertain me, and lots of opportunities to make something impressive of myself. It would be a great chance for a fresh start, not just for this situation but for me and you in general." Jovan loved her so much that it didn't matter where she wanted to go; he was going to be right by her side regardless.

Nicole couldn't help but feel overwhelmed with anticipation and angst about how all this would play out, but she knew she was ready to take that step forward and finally capture the life she wanted and she knew she deserved. She placed a very passionate kiss onto Jovan lips and then smiled from ear to ear and let him know that she was ready for it all. He very gently stroked her cheek with his left hand and glared into her eyes and nodded back, indicating that the plan was in motion.

Chapter 8

THE FOLLOWING DAYS began with an eerie tone. Nicole awoke with a sense of heavy anticipation for what she knew was about to take place. However, as nervous as she was feeling, she was equally excited and ready to remove this black mark from her life and finally move on. She left the bedroom to find Jovan in the kitchen already dressed and preparing breakfast. "Damn, you're awake early?" Jovan continued cooking as if he hadn't heard anything that she said. "Are you listening?" Still he continued moving as if her words weren't reaching his ears. He was clearly in another place with his thoughts. Nicole walked over behind him and slowly tapped him on his right shoulder.

"Jovan, are you all right?" she asked. Finally, he turned around to answer her while making sure to avoid her eye contact, first drifting to the floor then up to the ceiling. Nicole reached out with both of her hands, placing them on both sides of his face and directing his eyes down to hers. "Seriously, why aren't you talking to me?" "Y… yeah, I'm all right. Sorry, I was just thinking about something. I didn't mean to ignore you. Would you like anything to eat?"

Nicole paused for a second, considering if she would just let his behavior slide. "It's fine, but tell me, what's got you so distracted?" The room went silent for a moment, then Jovan opened his mouth to reply. "I guess it's just this day, you know? I mean, I get that it's something you feel we have to do in order to finally start our lives together. I also get that I promised you I'd be there for you with whatever you needed." Nicole slowly removed her hands from his face then proceeded to take a few steps back. "Okay, so what's the issue then?" "The issue is, we are about to take someone's life and pin it on someone else. It's just a lot to handle and a lot to process. Neither of us has ever done anything like this before. Are you sure you can live with yourself after doing something like this? Isaiah did you wrong, and Keisha is no better, but these are lives that we are about to change forever. Maybe we need to take a step back and really consider if this is the path that we want to take." Nicole took a few more steps back then walked over to the couch and sat down, letting out a long and frustrated sigh. "So you're really going to wait until the day to tell me you're having second thoughts about this? We agreed on this, and you're backing out on me? Don't tell me that you're full of shit just like he is."

Jovan walked over to the couch and sat down next to Nicole, putting his arms around her. "You know it isn't like that. You asked me to be with you on this, and I am, but we do need to make sure that this is what we are prepared to do." She pushed Jovan hands away then stood up looking down at him with anger pouring out of her face. "I am fully prepared for what I have to do, and if you aren't, I can do it by myself. Years of being taken for granted and then betrayed by one of my only friends, my mind has been made up. Now are we doing this or not?" Jovan stood up, taking a deep breath and putting his hands behind his head. "Yes, we are doing this." Nicole looked at him. "Good. I'm going to go shower and get dressed, and then we are going to finish this so we can leave tonight."

After finishing up, showering, and eating the breakfast Jovan had prepared in silence, the two made for the car and began driving to the hardware store. Jovan took it upon himself to pick out and purchase the poison they would use to kill Isaiah. After skimming the aisles for some time, he found a brand that he felt would effectively get the job done, an extrastrength brand of vermin poison guaranteeing fast acting results. The cashier claimed anything or anyone who consumed this particular substance would perish in a matter of minutes, which was just what they needed. Once back in the car, Jovan and Nicole began to lay out just how they would accomplish the job. "All right, this is how we have to get everything to play out. Isaiah goes to the gym every day from one to three p.m., taking with him his gym shoes, shorts, and his bottle of protein. We have to get the poison into that protein powder and make sure it's in there before he mixes and drinks it at the gym. Sounds simple enough, right?" Jovan paused for a moment then responded, "Yeah, but how are we going to get back into the house to plant the poison in his stuff?" A smirk crept across Nicole's face, reveling she knew something that he didn't. "That's actually the easiest part of the plan. Isaiah's dumb ass forgot that I know where he keeps the spare key, so we won't even have to break in—well, at least not technically. Only one issue is getting him out of the house so we can get inside." Jovan sat back with a pleasant look. "Yeah that's true. Well that and our alibi." Nicole looked puzzled for a moment. "Alibi?"

"Well, yeah, we need someone to see us somewhere away from the house so if things go wrong, we can prove that we were away from the scene and had nothing to do with the crime, get it?" "Right," Nicole smiled at the thought of a good idea. "So wait, how exactly are we going to be away from the scene if we have to plant the poison?" she then asked. "Well, we can't be two places at once, and involving anyone else in on this increases the chances of us getting caught, so looks like we are going to have to go in while he's there and get out before he can see anything is up. Also, we have to get Keisha over to the house one last time before he leaves to prove that she was the last one near his stuff before he died." Nicole's look of satisfaction faded into a look of annoyance. She started to think that this was actually more work then she anticipated. Hell, at this point, all she wants to do was get it done and over with. "Do we really have to do all this?" she asked. "Yes, it's a murder. What exactly did you expect? If we don't cover our asses, we will end up in jail, and that's not something I'm trying to have happening. We do it right and leave nothing to chance or don't do it at all." Nicole reluctantly agreed. "Now look, this how we are going to do it. You get me the key, and I'll go in to plant the stuff. And while I'm doing that, you call Keisha and give her some phony congrats on the baby." "Wait, she never told me that," Nicole said. "Of course, she didn't. It's just to piss her off at Isaiah, remember?" Nicole shook her head yes but still looked kind of lost. "Really rub it in and make sure she gets as upset as possible, and then tell her that you heard it from Isaiah. Once she's angry enough, she will be ready to speed over to his house to confront him about it, then we will move in and plant the poison before he leaves out. A few neighbors will hear the arguing and see her leaving out, and that'll be all we will need to pin her there at that time. While he's distracted, I'll sneak out the back without anybody seeing and head straight for the mall or restaurant or somewhere crowded so people can see me. Before you know it, we will then get the call that Isaiah has dropped dead at the gym. What do you think about that plan?" "Well, damn, if I didn't know any better, I would have thought you worked on law and order or some shit like that." Jovan rolled over laughing. "Glad you like it. Well, if that's everything we need to get moving, we are going to make this all happen today. Oh, and one more thing, we need to wait a few days before trying to leave town just to make sure we don't look like we are running right after he dies. We wait a week or so, and once they've locked up Keisha, then we can leave." Nicole sang, "Sounds like a plan to me." Jovan started the car, pulling out of the hardware store parking lot and headed for Isaiah's house.

Chapter 9

As Nicole and Jovan pulled up to Isaiah's house, Nicole couldn't help but get butterflies in her stomach from the anticipation. She pulled down the sun visor and pulled her wavy long hair into a ponytail and tied it to the back. She looked at Jovan as if he was about to start barking out orders for her to do. He looked over and asked where the spare key was hidden. She looked over toward the tree and pointed over there. He laughed at her and asked if she could be a little more specific. "Oh, I'm sorry, just a little nervous, but the key is in that little hole at the bottom of the tree in the backyard." "Good. I can go grab that and then go in through the back door." "Well, in the meantime,

I will be calling Keisha to try and get her to come over." "Okay, go ahead and make that call. I'm going to run over there and grab the key. I'll be right back," he told her. After Jovan closed the door, she began to call Keisha. The phone rang, and on the fourth ring, she answered. "Hello?" "Yeah, this is Nicole. And before you hang up the phone, I understand that you think it's me who spread the rumor about you, but it was Isaiah. He's the one who told me about the baby. In fact, I was just talking to him, and he is still saying it. I figured he was trying to rub it in my face. That is why I called you." Keisha didn't respond right away. It took about a half of a minute before she was yelling at the top of her lungs, "Your weak ass motherfucker! How dare you go around spreading rumors about me? I understand that I shouldn't have done what I did, but damn, I can't walk down the street without somebody walking up to me telling me shit I know you said. Besides, if Isaiah really said that, why would he come to the club and try to kill me, talking about I've been saying I'm carrying his child?" Nicole looked puzzled as she tried to think of a quick lie. "Keisha, that was not me that told him, I swear." She rolled her eyes as she said it. "Now what's really fucked up is the fact that you had sex with my man then called me so I can hear it then have the nerve to attack me about it. We all know that Isaiah is a fucking liar. That is why you never liked him, or so I thought you didn't. I just called you to let you know he also told me there is a camera in that light fixture right above the counter y'all was fucking on." Keisha took a deep breath then asked Nicole if she was serious. "Of course, he was so mad at me he told me about the camera. I guess to hurt me even more. But knowing him, unless you get that video, you could end up on the internet." Nicole hung up the phone with hopes that it worked.

Meanwhile, Keisha began to think that Nicole was lying, but somehow, there was still a 30 percent chance that she was telling the truth. Keisha grabbed her bat and car keys then headed for the door. "I'm going to get some answers today, whether I have to fuck both up or just him." She headed over there to see what all the fuss was about. Jovan sat in the car and let Nicole know he got the key and see how the conversation went. Nicole explained that she had to add to the lie because Keisha wasn't coming over just off the pregnancy rumor. Jovan asked what all did she say. "Well, I had to tell her that Isaiah had a hidden camera and was going to put it on the internet." Jovan looked at her with a blank stare, as if he couldn't believe she has added more to this mess. Nicole snapped at him, explaining that she had to do something. "Okay, as long as she is here within the next twenty minutes. Otherwise, we will lose our window." As Nicole and Jovan waited for Keisha to arrive, they spotted Isaiah walking toward his car with his things. "That's the worst thing that could have happened," Jovan said as he shook his head. As soon as he put the key in the ignition to pull off, they saw a car zoomed down the street and cut Isaiah car off. They all looked to figure out who it was. Keisha jumped out the car with a bat and started hitting his car and calling him names. Isaiah hopped out the car and began walking toward her so that he could grab the bat. The two of them caused a big scene, causing some of the neighbors to come outside and stand on their porch to watch. "This was not the type of attention I expected, but this is what we needed," Jovan said. Nicole then looked at him, saying, "This is the perfect time to go through the back door and plant the poison." "But don't we need the powder so we can pour it in?" Jovan asked. Nicole shook her head no. "That was the plan, but we have so many witnesses right now that if he dies tomorrow, they will still think the same thing. This is our only shot, so let's make it happen." Jovan crept across the street and went into the house through the back door. He ran right for the kitchen, where he found the container with the mix, and poured the poison in, then he got out of there. As he opened the door, he saw Nicole's eyes get big, and as soon as he looked back across the street, he saw Keisha trying to hit Isaiah with the bat and Isaiah running around his car to get away. Jovan put the car in drive and pushed on the pedal. "We have to get out of here and head over to her house so we can put the poison over there," Jovan said. "Good point," Nicole said as they headed that way.

Speeding around the corner fleeing from the house, Jovan accelerated in such a hurry he didn't realize he ran a red light. He felt they were in a hurry, and he knew he didn't have the luxury of proper driving at the moment. "Okay, we are out of their line of vision. Slow down before you get us pulled over and mess up any chance we have of framing her." Gradually removing his foot from the gas, Jovan began to slow the car down, making a swift right turn down a side street and heading for Keisha's house. "How much farther is her house?" Jovan asked while trying to remain as calm as possible and focus on the road. "It's not much farther. Make another left at this stop sign, and it'll be on the right side." Looking around for any oncoming cars or police officers who may have seen him peel into the side street, Jovan stopped the car at the stop sign then proceeded to turn and park the car on left side of the street. "Not right here. Keep going. It's at the end of the blocks," Nicole told him as she surveyed the area to see if Keisha's neighbors are around to witness. "If her house is the one we are going into, I don't want anyone to mistakenly see my car parked outside, so I'll stay here and you walk up." Nicole shrugged in agreement and proceeded to rifle through her purse for her friend's spare key and the poison they'd be using to frame her for the crime. "She should still be tied up with Isaiah and that situation, but don't take too long inside her house. Remember, plant it somewhere that she would normally miss but a cop would be likely to catch." Nicole closed the car door, nodded in Jovan's direction, and she walked away from the car and onto the sidewalk.

Keisha's block was usually pretty lively, but today for some reason, it was dead silent, which didn't bother her any. The less people around, the less likely she was to get caught. When Nicole finally made it up to Keisha's doorstep, she took one more look around to ensure that no one had seen her enter. She then proceeded to put the key in the lock and walked inside. Keisha stayed all the way on the third floor in a one-bedroom studio that was pretty roomy with plenty of places for her to hide the stuff, but the question was where. After making it up three flights of stairs, giving herself plenty of time to think it over, she decided that she would put the small bottle of rat poison inside a box but position it in a spot where it could be noticed. Nicole knew that her former friend never ate at home and was highly unlikely to look inside or even crave a bowl of cereal. She opened her front door, closing it nearly completely behind her then making her way past her living room and into the kitchen. Her television has been left on, and clothes were scattered across the floor. Nicole assumed from the rush that Keisha had been in to leave out and go look for Isaiah after hearing what he had been saying and doing. She walked into the kitchen and reached for the cereal on top of the fridge against the wall. Even standing on her toes, she wasn't tall enough to reach it, so she knew she had to go find some kind of stool or stepladder to stand on. Looking around the apartment, she couldn't find nothing to stand on; it seems as if Keisha had moved around some things since the last time Nicole lived there. Eventually, she said "Forget it" and dragged a chair across the hardwood floors but tried her best not to make too much noise. It was at that moment that Nicole heard the sound of a door creaking open and an older woman's voice call into the apartment. "Keisha? What's all that noise you're making in here?" It was Keisha's neighbor who stayed on the floor under hers. Nicole had to act quickly or risk the entire plan blowing up in her face. She jumped down from the chair and walked over to the door to greet the woman. "Oh, hey, Mrs. Johnson, how are you?" Nicole tired her best to wipe the guilty look off her face. "Hey, Nikki, how have you been? I haven't seen you around in a little while now. I figured you and Keisha might have gotten into it." A drop of sweat slid down the side of Nicole's face. "I'm doing all right, and no, me and Keisha are fine. We both just been busy, so I haven't had the time to swing by, but she was in a rush earlier and forgot something, so I came to grab it." Nicole had hoped her story was making sense as she continued to let the words spill out of her mouth as fast as her head could crank them out. Mrs. Johnson just smiled as she looked around the front room of the apartment, which was visible from the doorway. "Yeah, that girl is always in a rush somewhere. No wonder she forgets things. Did you want to borrow our ladder? My lazy husband could bring it up for you." Nicole quickly pondered the idea then decided it would probably be best to decline the offer. "No, thank you. I don't want to put you through the trouble. Besides I already got it down." Mrs. Johnson said goodbye then headed out the way she entered. Nicole then hurried to put the poison in the box then put it back on the fridge next, moving the chair back; and darted toward the door, locking it behind her; and started running down the stairs, slowing to a fast-paced walk once on the outside. Nicole flagged down Jovan and signaled him to drive around the block and pick her up on the next street.

Nicole jumped in the car once she had seen Jovan park. "So how did everything go inside?" Nicole hesitated before answering then looked out of the window as the car headed down the block and back onto the main street. "Well, there was a problem. The next-door neighbor walked in on me." Jovan pulled the car over and shut off the engine. "This is not what we need. Now tell me what happened." Nicole let out a long sigh then looked in Jovan's direction. "Her neighbor heard me dragging the chairs and came up to see what was going on, and she saw me, but she did not see what I was doing. So I pulled some lie out of my ass and said that Keisha sent me over to grab something for her. She stayed in the front door and didn't come inside, so everything should be fine, so just calm down." Jovan let out an angry groan then slammed his fist onto the dashboard. "Calm down!" Nicole yelled. "You got caught by the damn neighbor, and you're telling me to calm down? Do you realize we are facing life in prison for murder if we get caught? This isn't the time to be calm." Nicole couldn't help but jump at the sound of Jovan's hand smacking the dash and jerked in her seat. "Okay, yes, I know it isn't the best position for us right now, but yes, it'll be fine. She knows me, and she won't go to Keisha about it. She will believe what I said, so yes, just calm down." Jovan didn't speak for a moment, and he looked out the window with his hand gripping firmly on the steering wheel. "Are you absolutely sure that she isn't going to say anything to Keisha? Because if she does, you and I are really fucked." Nicole halted for a moment, thinking to herself, and she decided she was sure. "Yes, it will be fine, trust me." Jovan's grip started to loosen around the wheel, and he sat up in his seat and turned the car engine back on. "All right, I trust you," he said as he checked his mirror and pulled the car out of parking and back onto the street.

The car ride to the restaurant after completing the tasks at hand was silent. Both Jovan and Nicole had separate thoughts going through their heads. Jovan began to question if agreeing to this murder plan was the best idea and wondering if maybe he should get out while he still could. The neighbor hadn't identified him, and he could just as easily leave Nicole to get caught on her own if things took a turn for the worst. However, his heart wouldn't let him entertain the thought for very long. He knew he loved Nicole, and whether she went down or got away with the crime, he was going to remain by her side. Nicole was sunk with guilt, wondering if she truly could trust the old neighbor to not go poking holes in the story and go to Keisha and accidentally informing her that she had seen her in the apartment. She accepted it was out of her hands now and just had to hope it'll all work out. Jovan pulled the car into the parking lot of the restaurant and parked, now reaching out for Nicole's hands before she could open her car door. "Look, I'm sorry for yelling. I just don't want to see either of us go down for this, and I'm trying my best to get this done as quietly as possibly, but I know you had no control over the neighbor showing up. You forgive me?" Nicole's face couldn't hide the smile that slowly took over her face as Jovan spoke and gripped his hand with her own. "Yeah, it's fine. I understand. At this point, we are all we have, and we can't afford to be at each other's throats."

She leaned in and planted a kiss on his lips before smiling again and getting out of the car.

"So how long do you think this will all take, for everything to play out I mean?" Nicole asked, eyes wide open. Jovan didn't answer right away, looking somewhat puzzled as he searched through her car. Nicole noticed that he was not paying attention, so she poked her head in the car door and asked what was wrong. Jovan's look of confusion had turned into a look of worry as he riffled through the middle compartment of the car then looked under the seats. "Shit!" Jovan whispered, just loud enough to catch Nicole's ear. She then walked over to the driver's side of the car to question what has Jovan so upset. "Okay, serious, what's the problem?" she asked. Jovan ceased the search and stood up looking over to Nicole. "I can't find my wallet. I think there is a small chance I might have dropped it in Isaiah's house." She froze for a moment as a sinking feeling overtook her stomach. "Please tell me you are joking because that shit is not funny on any type of level." Waiting for Jovan to confirm he was indeed playing a joke on her and realizing that this was not the case, panic took over her body, and she began pacing as her body shook uncontrollably. "You're really standing there telling me we both just pinned ourselves to this murder? What the hell are we supposed to do?" Jovan raised both of his hands and rested them on top of his head, trying his hardest to calm them both down. "I don't know. I don't exactly have a lot of experience with this murder shit. It must have slipped out when I was running around inside. Look, maybe we can go back and look for it, or even better, maybe he didn't make it to the gym. We might be able to get this back under control." It was at that moment Nicole's phone began to vibrate in her purse.

She walked back to the other side of the car and grabbed it before the buzzing stopped. "Hello?" Nicole answered, trying to maintain some level of control in her voice. The voice on the other end of the phone spoke, "Hey, Nikki, is this a bad time?" Nicole didn't speak, then the voice yelled hello again, snapping her back into reality. Nicole responded, "Sorry but, um, no, what's going on?" "Look, I know you and Isaiah weren't on the best of terms anymore, but I thought you should know. About an hour ago, Isaiah and I went to work out after some shit went down with him and that chick you used to be cool with. He was a little upset, but he seemed okay. After we ran for a little bit, he collapsed on the track. I called an ambulance and thought he was just working out to hard. They got there, and he wouldn't respond. He's dead. I'm not exactly sure what happened to him, but I just wanted to reach out and let you know." Nicole's world seemed to have stopped in time, and her body froze. She couldn't believe Isaiah was actually dead. "Nikki, you there?" the voice called out again. This time taking less time to respond, she answered, "Yeah, I'm here, just trying to process this. The people don't have any idea how he died? Was it light exhaustion? Tell me anything," she pleaded. The voice began to speak again. "They said it was some kind of substance in his system that might have stopped his heart. They just came out and talked to me. I'm still at the hospital now. No one have been able to tell what it was yet exactly." Nicole couldn't help but be surprised as tears started rolling down the side of her face. Jovan walked over to the passenger's side of the car and asked quietly what had happened, but Nicole made a hand gesture signaling him to hold on for a few more minutes. Nicole opened her mouth to reply, "So it was like drugs or something, huh?" The person on the other end then paused for a moment before speaking again. "They haven't figured it out yet, but they are going to do an investigation because shit isn't adding up. You know, Isaiah stayed working out and everything, so this was not something natural. Look, I have to go. His mother just showed up. But if I find anything else out, I'll give you a call." Nicole said okay and proceeded to hang up the phone.

Jovan looked down at her and asked again if she was okay. "What was that about? What's going on now?" Nicole eyes filled with tears as she told him that Isaiah was dead, making sure not to look in his direction. It was almost as if the world around her was no longer here, just her and the news that the man she used to love was now gone and by her own hands. "We have to get out of town," the words left her mouth as fast as they had entered her brain. "We messed up, and sooner or later, the police are going to put the pieces together, and we need to be gone before the trail leads back to us." Jovan didn't need to say anything. His response was written all over his face. He ran back over to the driver's side of the car and started the engine as Nicole hopped back inside, and he pulled out of the parking lot. "We aren't going to be able to take a plane like we planned, so I'm going to run you home in a few hours to grab all the clothes and stuff you need, and then we'll go and just drive for as long as we can, but we can't stay in this town." Nicole nodded as he sped down the main street and made a hard right. After a few hours of driving around to let things settle, they arrived at the house only to see a group of neighbors outside and the flash of red and blue lights. Police cars lined the right side of the block and were walking in and out of the house. "Shit!" Nicole yelled as she scanned up and down the block, trying to see what was going on. Yellow police tape had sectioned off the entrance and any type of opening to get inside. Before she could give the instructions, Jovan had already started reversing the car down the block and back onto the main street. "Damn, well, we are just going to have to head get a hotel room and think this out for a bit." They drove for about thirty minutes before arriving at the hotel that looked like a creep spot on the outside of town near a highway.

Jovan walked toward the entrance to go rent a room, while Nicole stayed outside trying to figure out how things got so out of hand so quickly. *Shit was so simple. All we had to do was plant the poison and wait for it all to blow up. I just wanted my life to finally be how I pictured, and now I'm at this sleazy-ass motel running for my life,* she thought to herself. Jovan walked back over to her with a key dangling from his right hand, trying his best to crack a smile as he looked at her. "I guess we lucked up they had one room left." Nicole returned the smile with a sarcastic look. "You call this luck?" The smirk Jovan was trying his hardest to maintain then fell. "It's just for tonight until we get everything under control. We are gone in the morning, but the house was too hot. Our room is the last one on the left side, 5B. Go in there and just take a breather for a little bit. I'm going to go fill up the car and grab us some food for tomorrow so we don't gotta stop for a while." Nicole let out a deep breath and reached out to take the key. "Okay, fine, just don't take too long. I don't like the look of this place and don't want to be here by myself." He smirked, but this one looked a bit different, almost as if something was floating through his head, but Nicole couldn't figure out what it was. She was so nervous and overthinking everything she just brushed it off. "I promise I will be right back," Jovan said as he kissed her forehead and proceeded to get back in the car to pull off. Nicole walked inside and headed toward the room.

When she first slid the key into the door, it didn't open, but after a few more tries, the green bulb by the door lit up and the door unlocked. She walked in, and just as she had thought, the inside was just as crappy as the outside. It was a twin bed with a red comforter that looked half made and a flatscreen TV riddled with fingerprints sitting on a small table; nothing else was inside the room. *This place was disgusting*, she thought to herself. She walked over to the brown couch on the opposite side of the room and turned on the TV to a movie she really didn't recognize. Before she had realized, she had drifted off into a nap. When she woke up, her phone began vibrating, alerting her that she had ten missed calls and four text messages.

However, it wasn't this that alarmed her, but the time that was displayed in the corner of her phone that read 11:45 p.m. It has literally been hours since she had arrived at the hotel, and there was no sign of Jovan. She immediately unlocked her phone and checked her missed calls, which were from him. Before she could press send and return his calls, another text message was sent to her phone. She pressed open, which led her to the conversation arch with Jovan. Her eyes started to water as she scanned down the list of messages that he had sent her over the last couple hours. He sent her a very long message that read,

> Look, Nicole, you know I love you, but this shit is just getting too out of hand. I didn't know what I was getting myself into, and now I just don't see a positive ending for this. We legit killed somebody and left evidence all over the place, and they are going to catch us sooner or later. I think we both need to just separate and run on our own to make things easier. I meant every word I ever said about my feelings for you and how bad I wanted the life with you, but sometimes, the things we want, we just don't get. With that being said, I'm leaving… I know your hate for me is growing as you sit there reading this, but I just didn't know what else to do. I'm so sorry, Nicole, and I hope that one day you can

grow to understand that despite my actions tonight, my love for you was and is real. I'll always love you, Nicole… Goodbye.

They say when love leaves your heart, you really do feel an ache, and Nicole felt exactly that. It was like a knife ripping through her chest. Her phone fell from her hands and onto her knees. While her body started shaking, she looked around the room and had no idea what her next move could be. It was at that moment she looked up and heard banging at the door. Shocked at first, she hesitated about answering it but tried to pull herself together as she walked over to the door, turned the nob slowly, and opened the door. A tall man in a brown shirt covered by a black trench coat stood there. "Excuse me, Nicole, I assume?" She paused for a moment then replied, "Yeah, my name is Nicole. What do you need? It's really not a good time." The man reached in his pocket and pulled out his wallet then did a flip of his wrist and revealed the badge on the inside. "Ma'am, my name is Detective William Brown, and I'm going to need you to come with me."

About the Author

MY JOURNEY STARTED in Calumet Park, IL., a hardworking suburb just on the outskirts of Chicago, where I was born and raised.

I was blessed to be born into a large family, anchored by loving parents who brought me and my eight brothers and sisters up, all with their own unique gifts and personalities. At times, it was difficult to find my voice, so I decided to speak through pen and paper.

This outlet led to my fascination with storytelling, imagining all the endless narratives and plotlines I would one day bind together and share with the world. All I needed was that spark of inspiration.

In my young life, I feel I've experienced so much. I've lived in other states, fell in love, worked all kinds of jobs, was a teammate on the court, and then a coach for the youth off of it. I am a sister by blood and a sister by friendship, a proud auntie to a new generation of our family, and now a full-fledged author.

All of this made me realize I didn't need a spark because my fire never went out, my stories were always within me; my successes and failures, my loftiest dreams and harshest realities were all waiting for their moment in the sun.

One of the toughest questions we've all been asked is, "Tell me about yourself"? Most of us answer by explaining what it is that we do for a living or what we like to do with our time. However, I don't think they have to be mutually exclusive.

I think who you are can be a combination of what you live for and what you do in your own time to fulfill it. For me, this is a new chapter in my life and I hope you too can turn the pages with me and reveal your life's narrative.

My name is Arnita Ingram, and this is my journey.

CPSIA information can be obtained
at www.ICGtesting.com
Printed in the USA
BVHW081321220421
605632BV00005B/586

9 781662 413094